"The world is a book and those who do not travel read only a page."

[SAINT AUGUSTINE]

NO BOUNDARIES
SPIRIT OF ADVENTURE

NorthWord®

NO BOUNDARIES
FORD OUTFITTERS

Foreword by Ed Viesturs & Introduction by Page Stegner

A TEHABI BOOK

TEHABI BOOKS

No Boundaries: Spirit of Adventure was developed by Tehabi Books and Ford Motor Company. Tehabi works with national and international publishers, corporations, institutions, and nonprofit groups to identify, develop, and implement comprehensive publishing programs. The name *Tehabi* is derived from a Hopi Indian legend and symbolizes the importance of teamwork. Tehabi Books is located in San Diego, California. www.tehabi.com

President and Publisher Chris Capen
Senior Vice President Tom Lewis
Vice President, Development Andy Lewis
Editorial Director Nancy Cash
Director, Sales and Marketing Tim Connolly
Director, Trade Relations Marty Remmell
Director, Corporate Publishing Eric Pinkham
Senior Art Director Josie Dolby Delker
Editor Betsy Holt
Production Artist Monika Stout
Copy Editor Laurie Gibson
Proofreader Lisa Wolff

Tehabi Books and Ford Motor Company wish to acknowledge the following people for their contribution in developing *No Boundaries: Spirit of Adventure*: Holly Beighley, Cathy Condit, Tracy Hill, Curt Jaksen, Steve Noxon, Chris Schembri, and Kaoru Seo.

Library of Congress Cataloging-in-Publication Data is available upon request.

ISBN 1-55971-825-0

The paper used in this publication meets the minimum requirements of the American National Standard for Information Sciences-Permanence of Paper for Printed Library Materials, ANSI Z39.48-1992.

First Edition
Printed through Dai Nippon Printing Co., Ltd. in Korea.
10 9 8 7 6 5 4 3 2 1

NORTHWORD

NorthWord Press is an imprint of Creative Publishing international (CPi). Since 1989, NorthWord has published top-quality books on nature, wildlife, and outdoor adventure. NorthWord publishes many of America's finest nature photographers and illustrators, and has a growing line of children's fiction and educational books.

NorthWord Press/ Creative Publishing international
President/CEO Michael Eleftheriou
Vice President/Publisher Linda Ball
Vice President/Retail Sales & Marketing Kevin Haas
Executive Editor Bryan Trandem

[TABLE OF CONTENTS]

FOREWORD

[by Ed Viesturs]

IT WAS TWENTY DEGREES BELOW ZERO. The unforgiving Tibetan wind whipped around me, covering the footprints of my passage—a constant reminder of the challenges that lay ahead amid the rock and snow. I scanned ahead, following the outline that defined the massive shard of glistening crystal. Everest. It stood taunting me once again, its spectacular crown sharply defined in the ethereal sky.

For years I'd thought and dreamed about climbing Mount Everest without bottled oxygen. It was the ultimate physical and mental challenge; one everyone said was nearly impossible. Three years earlier, in 1987, I'd almost reached the top. On the summit day, however, the weather turned bad. After years of training, months of climbing, and the top so close, I was tempted to continue. But I realized that although reaching the top seemed possible, getting back down did not. That settled it for me. Climbing has to be a round trip. So, not knowing if I'd ever reach the summit, I decided to turn away.

Now, after years of preparation, I was back at base camp and ready: well trained, prepared, focused. I'd visualized that final stretch of the summit ridge over and over. The summit had shadowed my dreams, my thoughts, everything. It would be the most difficult part, I knew. When climbing that high without supplemental oxygen, time races on while forward movement is slowed to a crawl.

Days passed. Days of numbing cold, incessant winds, and constant work. Nights of almost no rest, sleeping in tissue-thin tents and down-filled sleeping bags. Endless hours of plodding up a vertical mountain …until finally, I was once again three hundred feet from the top. I stared at the summit. A pattern emerged: one determined step, rest, a dozen breaths. Another singular step, rest, and more breaths. I focused on reaching closer landmarks. Each step became a goal within itself. And then, almost miraculously it seemed, I reached the top.

Those final steps, which I'd visualized for so long, were like a dream come true. I was on top of the world, and the experience was phenomenal. The curved horizon was defined by a serrated sea of mountains floating on a bed of clouds. I'd reached the cruising altitude of 747s! Even more, I'd achieved my goal; I was at the highest point on earth—and the reward was incredibly intense.

Since then, I've reached the summit of Everest a total of five times, and I'm now on a quest to climb all fourteen of the world's 8,000-meter peaks. This is a goal I've set to satiate my thirst for adventure. Climbing is all about the sheer beauty of being in the mountains, about the challenge and the thrill. It's about pushing my physical and mental limits, and achieving what I set out to do. Climbing is my passion, and I'll do it as long as I can.

Life is an incredible adventure—as it should and can be for everyone. So get out there. Go push your boundaries.

INTRODUCTION

[*by Page Stegner*]

FOR ME THE THEMES OF ESCAPE, EXPLORE, ENDURE, AND UNWIND are akin to the seasons of life. I hold among my earliest memories the long summer days on my parents' run-down old farm in northeastern Vermont. I would be out of the house the moment I could evade my mother's eye, and down to the brook that drained a swampy area below the barn. The brook flowed along a hedgerow dividing two hay fields before disappearing

into a tangle of chokecherry and puckerbrush, then wound for a quarter mile through a nearly impenetrable cedar wood to its outlet at the eastern end of Mud Pond. It was unbounded territory for a child to explore and teeming with wildlife—frogs, red squirrels, porcupine, an occasional fox, white-tailed deer, woodchuck—and often in the wet mud of a skidder road that ran through the woods, I found the tracks of moose, coyote, and black bear. In those days there was nothing calculated or controlled about my daily flight from the farmhouse and its association with rules, regulations, and orderly procedure. My impulse to escape and explore was utterly instinctive and spontaneous—as it is in all children—and it wasn't until I was a subadult that I began to think consciously about planned defections from the "civilized" biosphere. Later, as an adult (and often rather guiltily) I considered my time with a fly rod, cross-country skis, or a backpack as an imperative, a necessary release from the pressures and responsibilities of habitual life.

In my twenties and thirties I was inclined to transform outdoor diversions into asinine tests of endurance, too often measuring myself in terms of risks taken, classifications of pitches climbed or rapids rowed, numbers of miles logged under a forty-pound pack. In those days it was all about adrenaline and white knuckles. True, accepting a difficult challenge and persisting can intensify the experience and inspire a kind of joyful humility in the face of implacable nature, but it can also be a mere measure of testosterone. Happily I have gotten past my thirties. I no longer get high on physical exertion merely for the sake of intoxication.

Now I look on my time in the backcountry as a chance to unwind, to rekindle some of the childhood spontaneity that life has a tendency to flatten, to remind myself of things that really matter, like the sniff of pine-scented air, the taste of granite and ice in a snowmelt stream, pollywogs nosed into cascading water where the brook drops into a pool. Bread and wine in the wilderness. A calmer odyssey. ⏚

ESCAPE

[*Retreat* ✦ *Release* ✦ *Transcend*]

Escape **It is the impulse to flee, to leave the rat race behind for a while and reinvent ourselves in timeless space, that inspires us to cross boundaries and push beyond the edge. In a highly programmed, cybernetic world that renders us increasingly captive to our equipage, to our machines, computers, appliances, instruments, gadgets, and contraptions, we need more than ever the remission of escape. Call it what you will—wilderness, nature, the outback, or the West—wildness is where we retreat into the absence of our own noise, where we are able to turn the outward journey inward, and in so doing, with luck, find preservation of the soul.** [PAGE STEGNER]

"*HOME.* THE WORD CALLS UP
IMAGES OF SANCTUARY; A SAFE NEST.
BUT HOME NEEDN'T HAVE FOUR WALLS
TO FIT THAT DEFINITION. I LEAVE MY
WALLED AND MORTGAGED HOME FOR
ONE WITH A BLUE, DOMED CEILING AND
WALLS OF OPEN SPACE. MY REAL
HOME EXPANDS AS FAR AS I CAN SEE;
my arms reach out and
encounter no boundaries
—OR PERHAPS COME UPON THE SOLID,
TIMELESS ROCK THAT FORMS THE
KNOBBY BACKBONE OF THESE … HILLS."

[CATHY JOHNSON]

"THE KNOWLEDGE THAT REFUGE
IS AVAILABLE, WHEN AND IF NEEDED,
MAKES THE SILENT INFERNO OF THE
DESERT MORE EASILY BEARABLE.
MOUNTAINS COMPLEMENT DESERT AS
DESERT COMPLEMENTS CITY,
AS WILDERNESS COMPLEMENTS AND
COMPLETES CIVILIZATION. ...
We need wilderness whether
or not we ever set foot in it.
WE NEED A REFUGE EVEN THOUGH
WE MAY NEVER NEED TO GO THERE. ...
WE NEED THE POSSIBILITY OF ESCAPE
AS SURELY AS WE NEED HOPE."

[EDWARD ABBEY]

*"Surely in
the wild...we
can reinvent
ourselves
somehow,
found anew,
start afresh,
begin again."*

[ROBERT RUBIN]

RUNNER'S FLIGHT

[*by Pamela Hunt*]

THE AIR SMELLS SPICY, OF SUN-DRIED EUCALYPTUS and the sweet scent of yesterday's rain. Entering the cool hollows of the trail, I leave the sidewalk and land on rust-colored wood chips. It's quiet here—just the wind and the sound of my breathing. Shaded trees still drip with tiny bits of glass and the moistened earth clings to my feet.

The trail is bare in spots, slick like potter's slip, and I slide, mud slapping against my legs. It dries there, wind whipped, but I don't mind. I'm happy to have traded in my suit for shorts and a pair of Adidas. On the trail, my heart beats into my skin, and my mind wanders from the office, away from my nagging in-box, away from frustrations, discontent.

I round a narrow curve that overlooks a green canyon, inhaling the clean air and solitude. My footsteps fall into sync with each labored breath—a constant and reassuring rhythm. Looking out at the view I feel strong, unfettered. And though my pace is slow, I begin to fly.

I've found my self again, hidden here among the trees, and like a wood sprite, I duck in and out of shadows, dancing to the music of the birds and the thumping of my own footsteps. The self that is me is always here, waiting on the trail. She delights in my body again, finds freedom in this runner's flight, the space between motion and muscle. She tells me that I can run marathons and summit mountains, ace presentations and performance reviews. That there are no mistakes here on this trail as long as one foot falls in front of another.

And I believe her. I shout as I head down the flat path lined with trees steady as sentinels, perfectly ordered and at attention. Into the canyon I run, gliding through blotches of sun that dot the path and ignite the rocks with light. The cacti hang heavy with pomegranate blossoms, and rain puddles reflect flowers so yellow they don't seem real.

Under the space of the sky I throw my shoulders back and indulge my true self. The self that really matters. I run for minutes—hours?—until my lungs feel tight, wrapped like a wound bouquet. When the trailhead finally reappears, I stop, legs shaking with relief. Stretching out my tired muscles, I know my daily dance in the wind is over.

Even so, the air smells sweeter; I'm alive, invigorated, ready to rejoin the world. Yet the flowers aren't any brighter or the sky any clearer. Nothing has changed . . . except me. And that is all that matters.

*"Once on the mountain highway, once
the road rises out of these foothills and
serpentines about the scalloped slopes
of the mountains, things change,
sensations change, priorities change.
I change. I gather about me only what
seems necessary, fundamental;* I DELIGHT IN
WHAT IS BASIC—A COOL WIND; CLEAN, FAST WATER;
THE SMELL OF SWEET EARTH; *a fat trout in
water. There is an economy and an urgency
to life in the mountains, an immediacy
that defies exactness, the defined,
whatever is confined by rules.
In place of life's clutter, there is daylight
and dark and everything from joy
and exhaustion to fear coloring the
light, giving it substance."*

[HARRY MIDDLETON]

"TO RISE ABOVE
TREELINE IS TO
GO ABOVE THOUGHT...
IT IS TO FORGET
DISCONTENT,
UNDISCIPLINED NEEDS.
HERE, THE WORLD IS
ONLY SPACE,
RAW LONELINESS,
GREEN VALLEYS
HUNG VERTICALLY.
LOSING MYSELF TO
IT—IF I CAN—
I DO NOT FALL..."

[GRETEL EHRLICH]

"SOLITUDE SEEMS TO
*push the invisible
boundaries*
BACK EVEN FARTHER,
TO SWELL DISTANCES
AND CONTOURS."

[MICHAEL LANZA]

"IT'S THE PURE, FERAL *rush of freedom*—THE KIND OF LIGHTHEADED THRILL AND

UNCERTAINTY THAT A WILD ANIMAL MUST FEEL UPON BEING LET OUT OF A CAGE." [PETER OLIVER]

IN THE WHITE ROOM

[*by Peter Oliver*]

It is a sweet, strange sound, the crisp song of new snow. In the friction between skis and the sharp crystals of dry, midwinter snow comes a noise like a fraying bow drawn hesitantly across old cello strings. A soft groan, a muted creak—harmonic brilliance to anyone willing to be wooed by the enticements of the backcountry world in winter.

The sound of cold snow crunching under each stride on a long ascent is filled with the promise of a high-speed descent soon to come. The mind's eye envisions powder flying, heart pounding, skis burrowing, then levitating toward the surface of the snow, eyes bugging out with idiot joy—a downhill dance. That vision is the one constant in a potpourri of random thoughts stirred in the uphill procession, as unflagging as an incoming tide, toward some distant ridge backlit in the morning sun.

The basic equation of big-mountain backcountry skiing sometimes seems comically unbalanced. Hours of uphill toil for no more than a few minutes of downhill dancing. One ski sliding in front of the other a thousand times over in a hypnotic routine. Why bother? Yet the notion that the descent is the reward and the climb nothing but grunt work and sacrifice is misguided. Descending is all about speed and physicality—it's a fast-acting, fleeting intoxicant. Climbing, on the other hand, inevitably evolves into a meditative soul-search. If the descent is pure extroversion, the climb is introversion, and the longer the climb, the more complex, deep, and satisfying the tendrils of introversion that wind within.

Wintertime in the north creates an illusion of impassability. Snow falls, entombing the countryside in an impenetrable deep-freeze. Winter chases most people inside, where they remain like hibernating creatures, emerging only for life's necessities and pleading to the gods for an early spring.

But snow is liberating. Summer is the season that throws up barriers and impediments that make back-country travel laborious and cumbersome. Imagine the tundra bogs and willow thickets of Alaska; the lush, entangling forest floor of northern Minnesota; the Vermont meadows of tall grass and briars. No easy passage there. But snow falls in winter, and the bogs and streams freeze, the forest undergrowth goes dormant, the meadow grasses lie down. With a sturdy pair of skis and, if necessary, climbing skins, it's possible to go pretty much anywhere. Shame on those cabin-fevered sluggards. Snow is opportunity.

And so stories come from all over, sometimes wildly imaginative and crazy stuff: hardy folk skiing across the poles, or traversing the entire 2,000 miles of the Yukon River, or climbing and descending the fiercest peaks of the Alps. Entry into the winter backcountry, regardless of the region of the world, becomes a revelation into how snow and ice can transform the environment into a work of art. The aquamarine blue of glacial seracs in the high mountains, evergreen branches supporting mushroom tufts of fresh powder, needlepoints of refracted sunlight captured in the surface of the snow—winter never falls short in its ability to deliver visual stimuli.

Almost anything is possible in the winter backcountry, and it needn't be heroic or expeditionary. Simply meandering in the forested hills of New England or scrambling around the Colorado high country is enough—backcountry skiing is whatever anyone chooses to make of it. Ambitious, whimsical, boldly athletic, contemplative, seemingly suicidal— pick a theme, any theme. If there is a common sentiment among backcountry skiers, it is probably some

real or imagined need for distance from the intrusions and anxieties of the familiar world. Behind in the snow extends a zipper-like line—a recorded imprint of the journey already traveled and a symbolic, umbilical connection with the world left behind. It is a connection that ever so gradually dissolves as a full, sensual immersion in the winter backcountry takes hold.

It is not always perfect. The wind screams; frostbite and hypothermia are persistent menaces; crevasses, cliffs, and cornices threaten. In the windblown snow or fog, or in the pall of new-falling snow, getting lost is a reasonable prospect, and an avalanche could be hidden in any snowpack. Winter can be a mean and petulant host, and though every season harbors its cruelties, winter's moodiness can be especially punishing.

But winter is also the purest of seasons. After a fresh snowfall, the landscape is newly created, covered in a chaste blanket of white. When the morning light sweeps cleanly across a swath of new snow, when the air is still and the temperature cold but tolerable, when each stride forward breaks new ground, it is easy to imagine, in the untracked snow, that one has embarked on a journey entirely original, into a world where no soul has gone before. It is then that the snow, with its muffled squeals and groans, breaks into song. ⚑

"YOU VISIT THE WOODS OR THE
MOUNTAINS OR THE SEA IN YOUR
VACATION. YOU LOAF ALONG TROUT
STREAMS, OR IN RED AUTUMN WOODS
OR CHASE GOLF BALLS OVER GREEN
HILLS, OR SAIL ON THE BAY AND GET
BECALMED AND DO NOT CARE. FOR THE
PLEASURE OF LIVING OUTDOORS YOU
ARE WILLING TO HAVE YOUR EYES
SMART FROM THE SMOKE OF THE
CAMP FIRE, AND TO BE WET AND COLD
AND TO FIGHT MOSQUITOES AND FLIES
YOU LIKE THE FEEL OF IT, AND YOU
WAIT FOR *that sudden sense of
romance everywhere* WHICH IS
THE TOUCH OF SOMETHING BIG AND
SIMPLE AND BEAUTIFUL. IT IS ALWAYS
BEYOND THE WALLS, THAT SOMETHING.
BUT MOST OF US HAVE BEEN BULLIED
BY THEM SO MUCH THAT WE HAVE
TO GO FAR AWAY TO FIND IT;
THEN WE CAN BRING IT HOME
AND REMEMBER."

[EDNA BRUSH PERKINS]

"AND SO I HAD ARRANGED TO SPEND SEVERAL

DAYS IN THE MOUNTAINS, ALONE,

WITH NO PARTICULAR GOAL AND NOTHING TO DO.

NO WALKMAN, NO BOOK. JUST ME AND MY

JOURNAL ... WHAT HAPPENS IN THE WOODS IS THIS:

The mind is forced to deal with certain

niggling but elemental details.

THOSE THINGS WE TAKE FOR GRANTED—

SHELTER, FOOD, BASIC CONVENIENCES, COMFORT,

BRUTE SURVIVAL—REQUIRE ALL OUR ATTENTION

AND MUST BE ATTENDED TO. WHEN A STORM

IS BLOWING IN AND THE TENT ISN'T SET UP,

worrying about mortgages and outlines

is a luxury. LATER, SUCH CONCERNS SEEM

AN IMPOSITION. PRIMITIVE NECESSITY, IT SEEMS,

CAN SNAP THE THREAD OF LINEAR THINKING."

[TIM CAHILL]

*"I would like
to learn, or
remember,
how to live.
I come to
Hollins Pond
not so much to
learn how to live
as, frankly, to
forget about it."*

[ANNIE DILLARD]

"*Destinations change like fashions and should not be taken too seriously.*

Explore **As a child I was endlessly captivated by narratives of discovery: accounts of the polar expeditions undertaken by Perry and Scott, La Salle's exploration of the Mississippi Basin, the journals of Lewis and Clark. But I could never fully accept the motivation behind these fantastic adventures—the mumbled explanations that they were undertaken in the interests of science, national pride, territorial acquisition, or, better yet, Edmund Hillary's famous reason for his first ascent of Mt. Everest: "Because it was there." None of these seemed more than partial truths. What really drove these men to such lengths of endurance and suffering? In time, my own far more modest forms of exploration down Southwestern rivers and into uncharted areas of the Sierra Nevada taught me that the compelling force has as much to do with a hunger for self-discovery as it does with any innate curiosity over what lies beyond the next hill. Inquiry into the natural world is also an investigation of the subliminal self, and it is what we find out there in back of beyond that reflects our individuality.** [PAGE STEGNER]

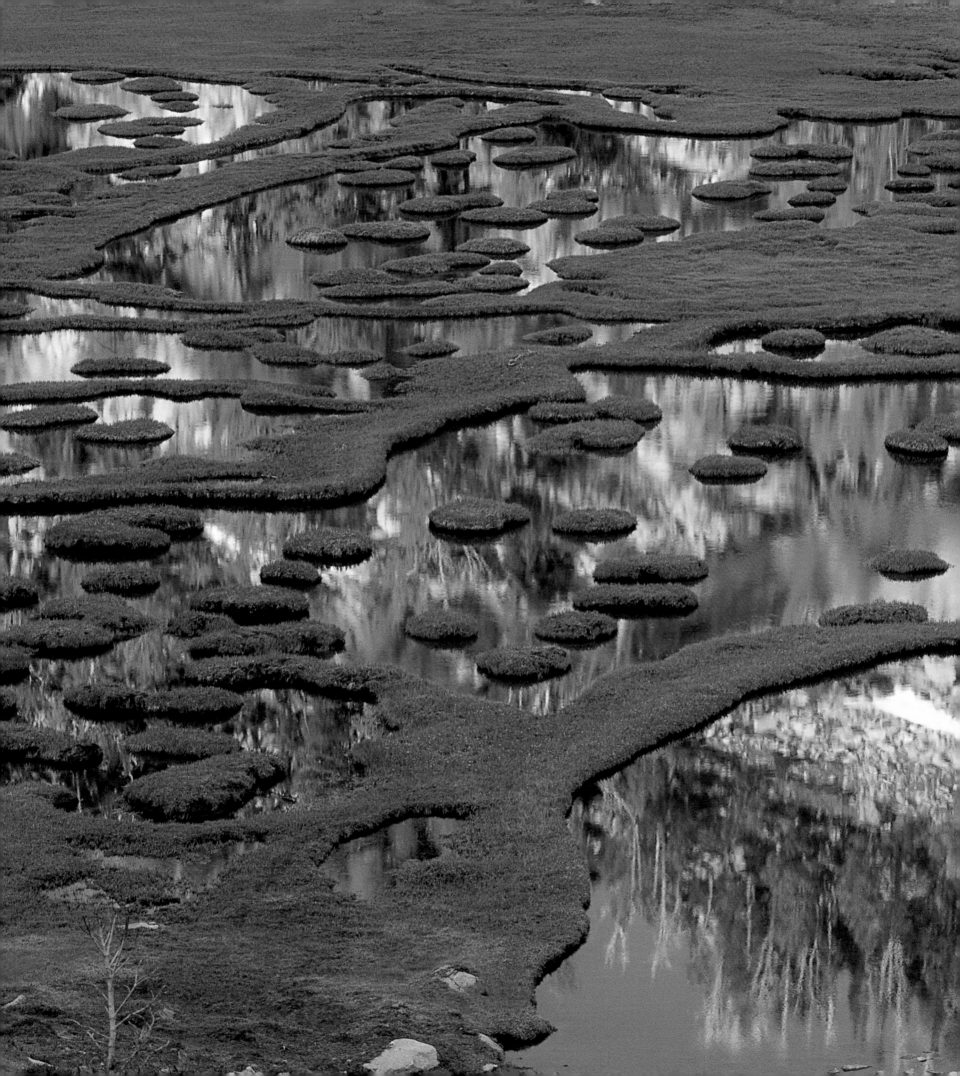

"THOUGH WE TRAVEL
THE WORLD OVER TO
find the beautiful,
WE MUST CARRY IT WITH US
OR WE FIND IT NOT."

[RALPH WALDO EMERSON]

"Most of my wandering in the desert I've done alone.
Not so much from choice as from necessity—I generally prefer to go places
where no one else wants to go." [EDWARD ABBEY]

"*We shall not cease from exploration*
and the end of all our exploring
will be to arrive where we started
and know the place for the first time."

[T. S. ELIOT]

"THERE IS SOMETHING MAGICAL ABOUT

AN OPEN FIELD OF UNTRACKED SNOW.

IT BECKONS YOU, AND BEFORE YOU

KNOW IT YOU'RE HOWLING IN DELIGHT

AS THE POWDER LIGHTLY GLIDES OVER YOUR

HEAD AND SHOULDERS. *When you come*

to a stop, you proudly turn back

to see your tracks—THE FIRST TO

BE ETCHED IN THIS PRISTINE SETTING

YOU WORKED SO HARD TO FIND."

[MAGGIE OBERWISE]

THE GIFT

[by Jeanhee Kim]

My first breath underwater is mesmerizing. As I sink away from the sound of the boat's engine and crashing waves, I am enveloped by clear blue water that is so warm, I can descend sixty feet without a protective wetsuit. Bubbles trail from my regulator as I carefully breathe in and out, ever mindful of conserving air for the dive ahead.

This is one of my first scuba dives since being certified, and I cannot get past the numbers, rules, and warnings. I check my depth and air gauges to monitor my progress:

twenty feet…thirty-five feet…fifty feet…three thousand pounds of air.…I float by a world that is mostly gray coral reef, with yellow tube, purple and orange fan, and chalky-white brain coral breaking up the monotony. The landscape is stretched so long and wide it seems I have entered a silent and desolate world.

With a light flutter kick, I catch up to my diving partners. Like schools of fish, we explore together, but each in our own world. As we pass over an outcropping of coral I spy a dark pattern on the sandy floor. Something is moving, half-hidden near the sandy bottom. A sea turtle! Her head pokes out from

under the reef, as if she were engaging in a game of hide-and-seek. My throat tightens. Treading gently with my arms to keep a respectful distance, I study her ancient, heavy-lidded eyes and hard, worn shell. Even the edges of her fins are frayed. How old is she? Fifty? One hundred?

She rises up to where I hover, and stares at me, unblinking. Unafraid. Awestruck, I feel solemn, vulnerable, alive. I'm face-to-face with an animal whose day-to-day existence I can't imagine, floating in an environment that without tanks, tubes, and masks is inhospitable for human life. My breath vibrates loudly in my ears, intensifying the feeling of solitude, and for a moment, I fancy that I am an astronaut, an underwater explorer.

Another minute passes. Then, just as suddenly as she appeared, she decides to go. Her short, thick legs kick into action. She gains speed, and with the silent dignity of an empress dowager, swims away.

Once she has retreated into the shadows of the sea, I rejoin my friends, still flush from my unexpected encounter. It was purely by chance that I had spotted the ancient sea turtle, and I wonder: What else have I missed in my dives? Why have I been in such a hurry, so focused on gauges, performance, and details?

I drift lower to the sandy bottom, letting the current, rather than my fins, move me. The reef which just minutes ago appeared colorless to me now seems

to blossom with sea life. Blue and yellow angelfish, with their cantaloupe-scaled sides, swim low in the shadows. Orange-and-white clownfish and half-magenta, half-yellow fairy basslets dart their inch-long bodies through the fan coral. Soft fronds of pink sea anemone dance to and fro in the current.

A signal from our divemaster breaks my reverie. We're down to 500 pounds of air; time to begin the long, careful ascent. First, though, I crane my neck hoping to catch sight of the sea turtle. She has vanished, of course. But my eyes have been opened, and I know that sea life is all around me, waiting to be discovered. Green eels are poking their heads out of crevices; shrimp and lobster are hiding in caves; manta rays are burrowed in the sand. Reluctantly, I point myself upward, and thank the sea turtle for her gift. ⚏

"OFTEN THE PLACES
[PEOPLE] REMEMBER ARE
NOT THE NAMES THEY FIND
ON THE MAPS. IT IS THE
little nameless waterfalls
THEY HAPPEN UPON OR SOME
LITTLE CANYON THEY STUMBLE
INTO. IT'S NOT THE PLACES
SOMEONE TOLD THEM ABOUT
BUT THE ONES THEY DISCOVER
FOR THEMSELVES."

[DAVID MILLS]

*"One of my greatest surprises
[in my photography career] has
been finding especially wonderful
scenes in the most ordinary places.
I had expected to make my photographs
on mountaintops or in national parks,
not on the interstate or in vacant
lots. Even photographs I have
made in famous parks…have been
surprises, occurring in out-of-the-way
places, underfoot, and at unexpected
times. Many of them I could not
have imagined. Most have come
from a kind of 'sauntering,'
a wandering in which I follow
only my intuition."*

[JOHN WAWRZONEK]

"FOR MY PART,

I TRAVEL NOT TO

GO ANYWHERE,

BUT TO GO.

I TRAVEL FOR

TRAVEL'S SAKE.

THE GREAT AFFAIR

IS TO MOVE."

[ROBERT LOUIS STEVENSON]

"The world cannot be discovered by
a journey of miles, no matter how long,
but only by a spiritual journey, a journey of one inch,
very arduous and humbling and joyful, by which
we arrive at the ground at our feet,
and learn to be home." [WENDELL BERRY]

WHAT LIES BENEATH

[by Melanie Beroth Dobson]

THE CRISP BLUE SKY DISAPPEARS FROM MY VIEW, and my eyes slowly adjust to the darkness. My ears strain for a sound—any sound—but find only silence. Relaxing, I let the solitude envelop me as I contemplate what lies below.

Cool air rushes on to my bare face, and I shiver, glad to have dressed for the occasion in my worn jeans, gloves, bright lavender bandanna that covers my head, and beat-up sweatshirt that has been scarred by the sharp rocks and corners in too many muddy caverns. My hands shake slightly—not from nervousness as much as from anticipation. I adjust the small lamp on my head, sucking in my breath as the light illuminates the rocky red walls of the tunnel. For a moment I forget the harness and rope that are slowly lowering me into a deep crevice of the unknown.

Tomorrow I will wonder why I spent my day crawling around in mud, scraping my arms and legs on rocks and ledges, and ducking bats that love to get tangled in my long hair. My muscles will ache and my knees and arms will be dotted with black-and-blue welts that show and tell. But my discomfort will be fleeting, and inevitably, I will close my eyes again and again to remember the cave and its quiet but startling beauty—its narrow, maze-like tunnels and dramatic, age-old formations.

It has probably been years since anyone ventured into this cavern. I discovered it months ago in the torn pages of an old library book. Intrigued by the description of its beauty, I lured my team to the spot, exactly where the author had directed—a simple hole in the rocky ground, folded into the steep Blue Ridge Mountain cliffs above a pastoral field filled with cattle.

Now my boots slide into the soft mud at the cave's front door, and I wait for the rest of my team to descend so that together, we can cautiously explore what is inside. The clay-like walls seep water from their pores, and a small opening in the wall beckons. I can hardly wait. The minutes seem to stretch into hours until finally, everyone touches down. Once we ensure each person is accounted for, we begin our journey into the cave, sticking together like a pack of wolves. Caving with a team is crucial; in the underground world, getting lost or separated from the group can be deadly.

Soon I am on my hands and knees, crawling down a long, slippery mudslide that leads from the cave's entrance. At the end there is a small, stale room with a dark, rocky ceiling tapered down to each of its honeycombed walls. I shine my light onto its center-piece—amazing! A turquoise-colored pool rests so quietly that we seem to be looking at its sandy bottom through a thin layer of glass. No one dares to disturb it.

Inching past the pool, I follow the group toward a small crevice at the far end of the room, and we discover a slim, winding tunnel inside. My muscles, skin, and especially my knees cry out as I push them through the claustrophobic space and over the piercing rocks that seek to leave their mark. The air is damp and musty and squeezes my lungs. But I press on.

I am rewarded with a maze of rooms, seemingly an endless catacomb decorated with slim ivory stalactites that hang like stained teeth, and huge boulders that beckon me to climb and conquer. Above, fossilized seashells have permanently embedded themselves in the cement-like ceiling, while below, the beam from my headlamp searches for the bottom of the steep ledge, but the light dissipates in the darkness. My shoulders tense, and I inch back. One slip, and I could plunge down a cliff that seems to have no end. Yet I still want to know what is below.

Behind every wall we find there is another room to discover, another level to explore, another tunnel to squeeze through. In the rooms, secluded corners are accented with colorful and crystallized stone that looks like a hidden treasure. Long passageways connect to other passageways. I feel like a schoolgirl playing house in this damp, brilliant place, and I wonder, Who has been here before? How long has this cave existed? My imagination wanders.

What I love most about caving is the mystery—not knowing what I will find around each bend and then discovering a new passage under an unlikely boulder or crevice. It takes me out of my busy but repetitious world and puts me in a place of extraordinary beauty and charm. What I discover is always unexpected—there is nothing predictable about exploring a cave, and I need to step out of my predictable schedule to realize there is more to life than pushing papers, paying bills, and meeting endless deadlines that seem so critical at the moment. When I'm down under, the stress of life disappears as I venture through this amazing and peculiar place.

With my group, I follow a stream that winds past rocky cliffs and pours into a tall, muddy chamber where it rushes over the side and crashes into a pool below. I want to know where the water travels from there—but our time has disappeared, and we must turn back before the outside light vanishes and strands us in this lonely countryside.

I strain to follow the water with my eyes, but the stream runs into the darkness. Slowly, I turn to head back to the cave's mouth, wishing for just a few more hours of uninterrupted discovery.

Climbing back into the world, I am momentarily blinded by the sunlight. As my eyes adjust, I see my teammates' faces, lit with smiles. I grin back at the others, exhilarated. Together, we explored a spectacular and meticulous world, tucked just beneath the earth. Few will be privileged enough to see this ornate creation, part of Mother Nature's masterpiece—and I experienced it firsthand.

My clothes are covered in dried mud, and my muscles are already starting to ache. Tomorrow I may be exhausted, but today I am happy. ◪

"There's something deeply satisfying about paddling the length of a lake, carrying your boat and gear over a trail worn smooth by the feet of the travelers who preceded you, and reaching lakes that are each less visited than the one before. Campsites are smaller, trails less trampled, the quiet more encompassing. We need quiet places, and we need quiet ways to travel in them. We never quite realize how valuable they are until we've been paddling, camping, and fishing in them for days. Once cleansed of the residue of daily living, it's possible to find what my son once called 'a calm spot' in your heart. It's a good thing to find."

[JERRY DENNIS]

"The only true voyage
of discovery, the only rea
rejuvenating experienc
would be not to visit
strange lands but to
possess [new] eyes...."

[MARCEL PROUST]

*"Two roads diverged
in a wood, and I~
I took the one
less traveled by.
And that has made
all the difference."*

[ROBERT FROST]

"YOU CAN SEEK OUT MOUNTAINS ALL YOUR LIFE AND STRIVE FOR SUMMITS AND ALL THE

TIME NOT KNOW WHAT YOU WANT OR WHY YOU DO IT, BEYOND THE BALD EXPLANATIONS OF THE CHALLENGE OR THE NEED

FOR SOME DIMLY UNDERSTOOD SENSE OF RENEWAL. SO FEW THINGS EVER SAID ABOUT MOUNTAINS

SEEM EQUAL TO THE INTENSITY OF BEING IN THEM."

[CHIP BROWN]

ENDURE

[*Focus* ✦ *Persist* ✦ *Conquer*]

Endure I have just come up from the Split Mountain take-out at Dinosaur National Monument after four days of wet, miserable rowing down the Green River in a howling wind and a driving rainstorm, stale English muffins and cold coffee for sustenance. I think nobly of myself for having faced the challenge, held out against the elements, persisted courageously and hung on against the odds. Though suffering mightily, I have survived the ordeal and conquered the environment. Old Shackleton crossing the frozen Weddell Sea has nothing on me. At least it's nice to think so. At best, we share two things in common—tenacity, and an addiction for the experience: for scrambling up desert buttes and scaling ledges to sit above the grandest vistas; for crawling into alcoves of rock-capped mountains; for trekking miles among venerable forests of ponderosa that tower over a hundred feet tall … For those of us, like Shackleton and myself, who suffer from the addiction, there is but one path. [PAGE STEGNER]

"FEW [PEOPLE]
DURING THEIR LIFETIME
COME ANYWHERE
NEAR *exhausting*
the resources
DWELLING WITHIN THEM."

[ADMIRAL RICHARD BYRD]

"Courage is resistance to fear, mastery of fear, not absence of fear."

[MARK TWAIN]

"RIDING THE BACK OF THE FLOODING

RIVER AS IT FLOWS DOWN INTO

A BEND, AND TURNS, THE CURRENTS

RACING AND CRASHING AMONG

THE TREES ALONG THE OUTSIDE SHORE,

AND FLOWS ON, *one senses the*

volume and the power all

together… IT CAN NEVER BE

REMEMBERED AS WILD AS IT IS, AND

SO EACH NEW EXPERIENCE OF IT

BEARS SOME SHOCK OF SURPRISE."

[WENDELL BERRY]

"A MENTAL SWITCH IS FLIPPED AND YOU EITHER WANK OUT AND

FAIL UTTERLY, OR YOU *face the challenge* HEAD ON." [SCOTT MILTON]

"I DON'T LIKE BEING COLD,

WET, TIRED, AND HUNGRY,

BUT THE IRONY IS THAT

BEING SO *evokes qualities*

of endurance I DIDN'T

KNOW I HAD, IT

CONCENTRATES MY

POWERS OF OBSERVATION

AND *intensifies the*

experience. IT

REARRANGES MY

RELATIONSHIP TO THE

NATURAL WORLD."

[ANN ZWINGER]

ALMOST HOME

[*by Bobbie Conlan*]

MY LOWER BACK ACHES, AS DO MY SHOULDERS AND ARMS, and my right hamstring—the one that hates to sit too long—is one enormous, fiery burn that is searing the back of my thigh. I rest the paddle across the cockpit and shift in my seat, taking my feet off the rudder pedals and stretching my legs. It feels good to be still for a moment and let the kayak drift.

Not for too long, though. We've been paddling into the wind for what has begun to feel like half my life, and I swear the beach we're heading for is getting farther away.

My clumsy stroke contrasts with that of my teammates Mark, Peter, and Pauline. They are adept, their arms a regular metronome, their hands rising right to shoulder level, textbook examples of how to paddle a touring kayak.

Up ahead—way ahead—a paddle flashes in the sun as Meph, first in our five-person team, catches a wave with a lazy stroke. So effortless. So efficient. Her stroke gives away her first love: outrigger canoeing. She has a high, angular spike that digs deep and breaks all the rules. But that spike—and her skill at reading the waves—has left us hundreds of yards behind.

This is also against the rules. "Stick together," Mark, our leader, had said yesterday as we began our ten-day kayaking and camping trip. Meph wants to push herself, though. If the rest of us were jogging, she'd be sprinting.

It's only day two in this marathon excursion, and I don't see how this novice kayaker is going to survive eight more. By the time we made our first campsite yesterday I could barely get out of my boat. But Mark has planned well. We didn't break camp this morning, so when we reach the beach tonight—if we reach the beach tonight— we won't have to unload the boats and put up the tents.

I pin my eyes on the blue hull in front of me and

try to match Pauline's rhythm. Lift, dip, pull . . . Lift, dip, pull. Her pale blue kayak contrasts against the sea of royal blue, and I wonder how many shades of the color exist. The Pacific is mesmerizing, its waters a purer, deeper blue than the changeable aquamarine around my native Oahu. So blue—and so cold! I shiver, remembering our safety exercises of the morning: capsize and roll out of boat, flip the boat over, crawl back in—and do it again. And again.

But that was ages ago. Now, late afternoon shadows stretch across the water. I've been paddling a total of eight hours, and every muscle and joint in my body is pleading for a break. Lift, dip, pull . . . Lift, dip, pull—*ouch*. My arm cramps, and tears pool in my eyes. I blink them away, embarrassed.

Then Peter turns to check on me, as does Pauline,

who gives me a shy smile and quick thumbs-up. Mark has actually dropped behind to shepherd me in, and I hear him say, "We're almost home."

Home: four small blue tents on a grassy patch above a curve of sandy beach. So simple—and welcoming. In the distance, I can see that Meph is already there, dragging her boat above the high-water line. As we pass between tawny yellow bluffs, the bucking ocean waters yield to calm bay, and my last few strokes to the beach are sweet. I coast in on a gentle swell. Meph catches the nose of my boat, steadying it as I climb out.

Mark, Peter, and Pauline guide their boats to shore, and together we stand on the beach, stretching our legs, watching the sky turn from blue to pink. Three days ago I didn't know any of these people. Today we are family. ◢

*"To find the real outback
you must abandon roads,
carry food and shelter on your
back, and walk. The best
walking is with family, friends,
and lovers. Take children
and dogs; take a camera.*
HIKE UNTIL YOUR BREATH FAILS
AND YOUR LEGS SEEM TO MOVE WITH
A WILL OF THEIR OWN. *Pitch
your tent as dark falls.…
Sleep under the stars."*

[ANNICK SMITH]

"SOMETIMES THE WILDERNESS CAN LEAVE YOU *reeling with joy*. SOMETIMES IT CAN MAKE YOU VERY, VERY HUMBLE." [JEFF RENNICKE]

EPIPHANY STAGE

[*by Rob Story*]

STEVE, KEITH, AND I WERE ATTEMPTING an all-day mountain bike traverse of California's Santa Ana Mountains—a ride that demanded seventy-plus miles of pedaling and 12,000 vertical feet of climbing, much of it on challenging singletrack. At four in the afternoon, we'd completed only two-thirds of the traverse, and our psyches as well as our quadriceps seemed as if they were filled with lead. The prior weekend, we had attempted the trek but given up thirty-two miles into it after a late start and a rash of flat tires. Now, deep into the canyon, shadows lengthened and—I imagined—cougars stirred awake, ready to pounce from the nearest bush. I entertained thoughts of coasting downhill, back to a pay phone to call for a ride home. Tempting . . . but despite my aching back and the miles ahead, I couldn't desert my buddies.

We rode deep into a canyon, following a creek. Then the trail hung an abrupt right across the creek and ascended one of the canyon walls. Ducking under low branches, we wavered unsteadily up a harsh incline littered with volcanic rocks. Even in our lowest gears, fluid riding was impossible. I grew resigned to dismounting regularly. Pushing the bike, I thought iron-ically, was good variety—a chance to let other, underused muscles cramp and ache, too.

After several minutes of this I mounted again and was churning up a cruel gravel chute when something in me snapped, chasing away the fatigue. In the middle of the chute was a crux: a steep-angled hump that couldn't be cleared without a well-timed and quite substantial weight transfer from back wheel to front. I planned to dismount for it. But Steve, who was in the lead, aimed left, narrowly avoided some overhanging brush, jammed down on his cranks, and swung back to the right just above the hump.

Maybe an endorphin kicked in at that precise moment, because I saw something unexpected and wonderful in that maneuver. As if the move were flint striking steel and I was a Cro-Magnon who had suddenly found a way to warm my furry knuckles. Some gut-level, pituitary-soaked emotion welled up inside and said, in so many words, "Dadgummit, we can beat this sumbitch." I cleared the hump, too, and felt oddly energized for the remaining six hours and thirty-odd miles.

If you're like me, you took your first real mountain bike ride years ago. Mine was at Wisconsin's Kettle Moraine State Park back in 1989. The park boasts an intricate network of trails, and every time a trail sign pointed upward, you followed it. Laps and miles and hours piled up until a couple of you bonked hard atop the biggest hill in the park. The bonk—the condition of going nearly hypoglycemic after hours of exercise—was a strange new phenomenon, and not altogether unpleasant. As you pedaled to a nearby grub shack for gargantuan pieces of rejuvenating apple pie—PowerBars had yet to infiltrate Wisconsin in 1989—you enjoyed a woozy sense of accomplishment.

To ride mountains, no matter how small or gentle, is to open your mind to . . . well, an open mind. That may sound vague, but how else do you describe the feeling of pedaling to a summit or overlook? How else do you categorize that heady mix of dopamine, pride, endorphins, free-ranging thought, delirium, and simple relief?

Up near the timberline in Idaho's Sawtooth Mountains, there's a famous shed with huge letters on the roof that prophesy: "The higher you get, the higher you get." I can't improve on that shed. Still, I've tried. The last time I crested a mountain pass on an all-day epic—the last time I got high on a bike, under my own steam, reveling in the power of muscle and will—I pulled out the little notebook I carry on biking trips and wrote the words "Epiphany Stage."

I wrote "Epiphany Stage" without looking it up, and the phrase could be inaccurate or silly or both. But if you've ever mountain biked till your head spun faster than your pedals, you know what I'm talking about. Because if you ride far and long and high enough, mountain biking transcends mere sport. It becomes a tingling fiber that runs from your gut through your heart to your brain and its various cognitive loops and pleasure centers.

Now I'm not a New Age hippie living in a fantasy world. But I do believe in head changes and a bike's ability to deliver them. I believe that, because of mountain bikes, the North American West has witnessed more transcendental experiences than the most holy Himalayan ashram.

By the time Steve, Keith, and I completed our traverse of the Santa Ana Mountains, we'd suffered two flat tires, one broken light, one mangled bike shoe, and skin abrasions galore. But none of that mattered. As we stood slapping hands under a cool indigo sky, one could almost smell the giddy enlightenment—I say "almost" because one could primarily smell three guys who had mountain biked seventy miles.

Anyway, we felt luminous joy and clarity. With every ridge we gained came a sort of spiritual summit as well. The mix of intense physical effort and umpteen hours of stream-of-consciousness thought intoxicated me for days. And when I finally came down, my bike was waiting there in the garage, ready to spin out new epiphanies. ◪

*"We are made
to persist.
That is how
we find out
who we are."*

[TOBIAS WOLFF]

"AFTER I GOT OVER MY FEAR, I STARTED TO [E]ASE INTO THE BEAUTY OF THE PLACE. WHEN YOU FINISH A CLIMB LIKE THAT, *all the stupid little fears* YOU CARRY [A]ROUND WITH YOU EVERY [D]AY SEEM RIDICULOUS."

[MICHAEL MCDERMIT]

"*We pull out into the current, back paddling to position ourselves before being swept over the falls. Though my heart is pounding, my breath is steady. … The front of the raft comes up and a solid wall of gray water comes pouring down on us from overhead. It feels as if we're capsizing end over end.* **I CAN'T TELL IF I'M IN THE BOAT OR OUT OF IT, AND THEN IN A SPLIT SECOND I KNOW THAT I'M OUT AS THE NEXT TWENTY-FIVE-FOOT WAVE ENGULFS ME, PLUNGING ME BENEATH THE SURFACE** … *Time balloons, full and swollen; seconds expand into minutes; there is only the gray thundering water, and my presence of mind. … Down, around, until the next moment, tossed up like a twig to the surface again. I am through the rapid. It has all happened within forty-five seconds. I look around and see that the paddle boat has not capsized and is just upstream of me, midriver, close enough for me to swim to. Somehow I still have my paddle in my hand. Someone grabs it, pulling me to the boat, then grabs me by the seat of my pants, frantically catapulting me back into the raft* …. **I AM LEFT STRIPPED, VULNERABLE, AND BARE. I FEEL TRANSPARENT, LIKE A CHILD, UNABLE TO DISGUISE MY FEELINGS.** *The pounding of my heart vibrates throughout my entire body. I am safe, there are friends holding me, laughing. I shake my head as though waking from a dream and let out a loud 'whoopeeee!'*"

[CHINA GALLAND]

"WHY GO THROUGH IT ALL? WHY GET FILTHY AND DIRTY AND SWEAT-ENCRUSTED?

I'M NOT SURE I KNOW THE ANSWER YET. THERE'S SOME KIND OF ELEMENTAL CONNECTION TO THE CYCLES

OF THE DAY: GETTING UP WHEN IT GETS LIGHT, WALKING WHILE THE SUN'S OUT, FINDING A PLACE TO

BED DOWN BEFORE IT GETS DARK, AND EATING DINNER AS THE SUN GOES DOWN." (ROBERT RUBIN)

UNWIND

[*Breathe* ❖ *Reflect* ❖ *Relax*]

Unwind **In the evening I hike to the top of Poison Spider Mesa and sit out on a point overlooking the imperial panorama that surrounds the town of Moab—the Colorado River a thousand feet below, Arches National Park to the north, Wilson Mesa rising abruptly from the east side of Spanish Valley, and the snowcapped La Sal Mountains backdropping the whole preposterous hallucination in alpine-glow pink. It is utterly peaceful and quiet, except for a playful wind that comes swirling at me like an attitude across the rim. It seems chipper enough, but a bit mercurial. Again and again, as I await its cooling kiss, I watch it whirling away from me and jumping from ledge to ledge. I am not much given to personification, but this wind, I think, is flirting with me: I hear her coming like black riffles across water, then flitting away again to boogie in the rice grass and yucca without so much as a peck on the lips. The temptress. I snub her next advance and she grabs my Charlie Tweedle imitation-beaver cowboy hat and flings it into the Jurassic void. Who cares. I came up here to unwind. Can't let your hair down if you're wearing a hat.** [PAGE STEGNER]

"Off in the distance
I hear rushing water.
Its cool mist lures me from
the hiking trail, away
from endless mile markers
and trail maps. Sliding,
struggling to keep my balance,
I force my tired and
sore legs down the ravine
until I spy the waterfall:
Its clear, burbling waters
are sparkling in the sun,
making music against the
river rocks! Moments
later, my boots are off.
I sink my aching feet into
the cold water, letting
it dance over my toes,
and lean my elbows into
the glorious mud. My eyes
close, muscles relax,
mind daydreams.
A perfect release."

[FRANCES LYNN FASSI]

UNSPRUNG

[*by Susan Zwinger*]

Traveling north toward Alaska, I have crossed into an otherworldly land called the Yukon. To escape from old-fashioned, hand-wound watch psyche that Europeans invented to chop time into short, cruel fragments, I go exploring. Whether it be the Yukon or my own backyard, it helps to search for something I love passionately— rainbow trout, wildflowers, minerals, or mushrooms. The key to destroying that tight little spring lies in allowing time for my senses to open like flowers.

Just before Whitehorse on the Alcan Highway, I discover something. Something so strange and so delicious, I must park and get out and walk with my head to the ground. Never mind that it is raining and cold— that's what rain hats are for.

If I did not get out of my truck, I would never discover such treasures. Such weather tempts me to keep going.

Within a few square meters of ground I find a form of drugless hallucination. I thought I knew tundra from backpacking over mountaintops in the Lower Forty-eight, but nothing prepares me for this delirium of spongy color. Mounds of peat moss, lichen, and liverwort swallow up my feet to the knees. Rosettes of rose, lavender, chartreuse, and rust bloom over lily frost-greens. Miniature neon-orange fungi spring up through the feathery lichens.

The world is inventing itself anew! This ground is so lush with moss and mushroom biodiversity that I cannot put my foot down without squashing something. Species of mushrooms glow purple and gold in the rain. Bright blue or red boletus—as large as dinner plates—

shock me with delight. Mushrooms are so creatively adapted to each and every temperature, altitude, and ecosystem, that they may exist nowhere else on the globe in this form. I am truly unsprung.

How peculiar is my eye: at first it sees nothing, then a little, and then a proliferation of forms. A lavender Cortinarius mushroom gleams slimy in the rain against the brick reds and greens of peat moss. What is it about the fungi that so grab the imagination? These spongy little wenches refuse the normal legged forms of fauna and the pretty symmetries of flowers. Unlike gravity's beasts, which must have legs or slithering bellies, fungi are unperturbed by such practicalities as grasping digits, heads and tails, opposing thumbs, and sense organs as we know them. Instead they ooze, loop, pulse, cover, reticulate, sprout, crenellate, drape, hang, and make themselves omnipresent any way they please. Laws of physics be damned.

Before me, elysian colors far beyond the known spectrum. Tomorrow the pleasure of cracking the code—I will pull out my guidebooks and search for their names. I glance up, rain trilling off the rim of my hat, and realize I am completely, entirely, unequivocally happy. I am down on my knees looking and I don't want to stop. I don't want to crawl into my truck and go to sleep. How can I close my eyes on such a magnificent world?

But for now, the night anchors bruised cumulus to the mountaintops and casts the lakes in bluish silver. I am at peace, at last, with my own company. I have crawled through the labyrinth of teeth inside that old watch, and popped out on the other side to be free. ⌘

"On still ... mornings, with
the lake so calm the surface
seems poised to shatter,
I always discover again the
pleasure of paddling for its own
sake.... A good canoe does not
merely travel across a lake or
river, it glides along the inter-
face between water and air,
making hardly a ripple
in passing, and is so silent that
it blends with the world.
Paddling it makes you part
of the lake, not an intruder, and
a participant in the
pastel dramas of dawn....
BEING OUT THERE IS NOT JUST
A WAY TO GREET THE NEW DAY, IT'S A
WAY TO BE REAWAKENED TO IT,
to see it again with the
eyes of children."

[JERRY DENNIS]

"THOUSANDS OF TIRED, NERVE-SHAKEN, OVER-CIVILIZED PEOPLE ARE BEGINNING TO FIND OUT

THAT GOING TO THE MOUNTAINS IS GOING HOME; THAT WILDNESS IS A NECESSITY;

AND THAT MOUNTAIN PARKS ... ARE FOUNTAINS OF LIFE."   [JOHN MUIR]

"HERE IN THE QUIET OF THE WOODS I AM TRYING TO TAKE STOCK OF ALL

THAT THIS YEAR HAS DONE FOR ME. IT HAS GIVEN ME HEALTH.

I HAVE FORGOTTEN ALL ABOUT JERKING NERVES AND ACHING MUSCLES.

I SLEEP ALL NIGHT LIKE A STONE; I EAT PLAIN FOOD WITH RELISH;

I WALK AND ROW MILE AFTER MILE; I WORK REJOICING IN MY STRENGTH AND

GLAD TO BE ALIVE. THERE HAS BEEN ALSO THE RENEWING OF MY MIND,

FOR MY STANDARDS OF VALUES ARE CHANGED. *Things that once*

were of supreme importance seem now the veriest trifles. THINGS

THAT ONCE I TOOK FOR GRANTED, BELIEVING THEM THE COMMON DUE OF

MANKIND—LIKE AIR AND SUNSHINE, WARM FIRES AND THE KIND FACES

OF FRIENDS—ARE NOW THE MOST VALUABLE THINGS IN THE WORLD."

THE PERFECT SECRET

[*by Jeremy Schmidt*]

NEAR THE MIDDLE OF A NEARBY NATIONAL PARK, protected by walls of wilderness, stands the perfect clearing. For me, it is a perfect secret.

It's not easy to get to. Hiking or skiing, it takes all of a long day, and sometimes more. There's no trail, only miles of bushwhacking through lodgepole forest—hard miles where deadfall chokes the ravines and boggy wetlands force long detours. Although I've been there many times, I've never followed the same route twice. I've tried. I've looked for a direct, repeatable way in, but something about the shape of the land, its lack of landmarks, the tangle of same-looking little creeks and hollows, leads me on a different path each time.

You could almost think it moves around, trying to stay hidden, a little pocket, a bubble of open space punched into the surrounding forest. No one else, as far as I can tell, has ever been there. It's as complete a secret as I've ever had.

It would be nearly impossible to find, except for the warm creek that flows from it. The creek cuts a crooked lane through the forest. Its banks are lush with overhanging sedge and bear grass, a stream of grass flowing through the dark trees. It looks like it would be easy walking but it's not. The ground is tussocky, squershy, and between the tussocks lie traps of black, oily muck. Best to stick to the forest, where the ground is hard, and follow the rivulet upstream.

I found it that way the first time, in January. Skiing alone across the park's great central plateau, I was following my compass under dull gray skies. With no landmarks, I had no clear idea where I was. The creek, when I came to it late in the afternoon, appeared only as an eccentric snow-covered road leading north-south. I thought how much easier it would be to follow it than to continue crashing through the trees watching my compass. But I needed to go east. Or I thought I did. I was young, and I hadn't learned that often the landscape knows better.

As I stood and considered the possibilities, I noticed steam gently rising from the snowbanks, and realized that a creek flowed beneath the pillowy white. A warm creek. That could mean only one thing. I followed it, and within half a mile, came to the clearing. A near-perfect circle, maybe an acre, not much more. A white expanse in the silent forest, and at its farther end, a mound of bare stony ground warmed by a hot spring.

The spring was a vent in the rock, a little bowl like a teapot without a lid. It sent out a small but vigorous stream of boiling water that ran down a channel for twenty feet to join the creek, where by some perfect accident of natural design, the mingled waters gathered in a tub-sized pool.

It was a welcome, almost unbelievable discovery. I was dog-tired from churning through deep snow since early that morning, and hadn't relished another cold camp in the endless jungle of pine. I set up my tent on the dry ground, pulled off my frost-stiffened clothes, and slipped gratefully into the pool. And stayed there. Didn't move, except to find the point where the temperature was perfect. Night brought a light fall of big, soft flakes that spun down invisible and silent around me, and it was late when I climbed into the tent for the night.

I go back there, when I feel the need, when life grows horns and needs taming. It's always a hard trip, and more than once I've had to spend a night out before I got there.

Yet, if it were easy, if it were a peaceful stroll through softly lit glades, it wouldn't be anywhere near as good. In summer, I arrive sticky with sweat and bug-bitten, flakes of pine bark down the back of my shirt, feet soaked from stomping through mucky sedge. In spring the snow rots from the ground up; you can't stay on top, even with wide skis. Winter is the best time, when the snow is deep and consistent, and smooths things out, yet even then parts of the route are rough and choked. The reward lies in the setting down of my pack and the relaxing of my tightly-wound self in a familiar and beautiful place.

Being immersed in this great forest, where for miles and miles you can see only yards and yards, is a sort of backward equivalent to blue-water sailing: You can't see far, but you can see a great deal. My clearing is an island in that sea of trees, a quiet pool in a vast green density. More than that, it represents a circle of calm in the larger turbulence of our self-inflicted modern culture. That calm stays with me even when I leave. Even as I thrash through the deadfall on the way out. ⚘

*"We need the tonic of wildness. ...
We can never have enough of nature."*

[HENRY DAVID THOREAU]

"WE ... PULL OUT A
COUPLE CHOCOLATE
BARS, DON WARM JACKETS,
AND STARE OUT AT THAT
MAGNIFICENT COUNTRY WHILE
THE LATE AFTERNOON
LIGHT TURNS MILES OF
SNOWFIELDS FROM CREAMY
YELLOW TO BURNISHED GOLD.
SUCH A PRIVILEGE IT IS
TO BE HERE. I ENTERTAIN
THOUGHTS OF EARNED
LEISURE, JUST REWARDS."

[JEREMY SCHMIDT]

"WE GO CAMPING TO BE *kissed by the wild.* FOR A BREATH OF TIME WE MAY THINK WE ARE ADAM OR EVE IN THE GARDEN WITH BEASTS. I STAND ON MOUNTAINS AND SEASHORES, OR BENEATH 500-YEAR-OLD REDWOODS, AND *I am humbled.* IT IS NOT ECSTASY I SEEK, ALTHOUGH ECSTASY IS ALWAYS WELCOME, BUT THE COMFORTING KNOWLEDGE THAT I AM CONNECTED TO THE LIFE AROUND ME."

[ANNICK SMITH]

"Therefore I am still
a lover of the meadows and the woods,
and mountains; and of all that we behold
from this green earth."

[WILLIAM WORDSWORTH]

"EVERY SUNSET WHICH I WITNESS INSPIRES ME WITH THE DESIRE TO GO TO A WEST *as distant and as far* AS THAT INTO WHICH THE SUN GOES DOWN." [HENRY DAVID THOREAU]

Sense of Place

cover
Monument Valley, Arizona
© Chris Sanders/Getty Images/Stone

A hiker contemplates the glowing beauty of Monument Valley, Arizona. This breathtaking preserve, located in the Navajo Indian Reservation, is noted for its incredible color and sweeping plateaus.

pages 2–3
Sierra Nevada Mountains
Galen Rowell/Mountain Light

A remote dirt road leading to Shepherd's Creek, beneath Mount Williamson in the Eastern Sierra, glows under stormy skies as it threads through California's high desert. At 14,384 feet, Mount Williamson is the second highest mountain in California.

pages 4–5
Southeastern Utah/Northern Arizona
Barbara Cushman Rowell/Mountain Light

Monument Valley's red- and orange-hued boulders, part of the vast Navajo Reservation, have attracted thousands of tourists since the turn of the twentieth century. Located on the border of southeastern Utah and northern Arizona, this twenty-five-mile stretch of canyon contains some of the most dramatic rock formations on the Colorado Plateau.

pages 6–7
Rocky Mountains
© Dugald Bremner/ImageState

Deep in Colorado's Rocky Mountains, a backpacker meanders through a trail strewn with bright gold autumn leaves and groves of barren quaking aspen. Named for the way in which their rounded leaves sway gently in the wind, quaking aspen cover the mountains of Colorado, casting the country in a magnificent bright gold during the fall.

pages 8–9
Sequoia National Park, California
Galen Rowell/Mountain Light

Campers wind down for the evening at a campground in Kern Plateau, part of California's Sequoia National Park. This diverse area is surrounded by designated wilderness—rocky trails, vast meadowlands, and open country—and boasts over 150 miles of marked trails.

pages 10–11
Big Bend National Park
Tim Damon

A late October sunset in Big Bend, Texas, casts the Rio Grande in a serene light. Big Bend National Park—named after the deep bend the Rio Grande has carved into the west Texas landscape—is one of the few national parks in the country where hikers and campers can enjoy uninterrupted, breathtaking solitude.

pages 12–13
Northern California
Galen Rowell/Mountain Light

The evening sky casts a peaceful spell over the waters at Shelter Cove on California's rugged north coast.

pages 14–15
Eastern Maine
Galen Rowell/Mountain Light

A thicket of trees laced with pumpkin-orange and red creates a peaceful setting on Deer Isle, Maine. The second largest of the state's coastal islands, Deer Isle is primarily a fishing town, with more than half of the community's population affiliated with the industry.

page 16

Tibet

© 1992 Charles Mace

Ed Viesturs and climbing partner Scott Fisher carefully traverse Bottleneck Couloir on K-2 at 27,000 feet. Just hours before, Viesturs and Fisher had nearly died in an avalanche while attempting to rescue two other climbers stranded near the summit. Viesturs saved himself and Fisher, who was roped to him, by arresting their fall with a pick-ax—seconds before they tumbled over a 7,000-foot cliff. After rescuing the other climbers, the two made a risky push for the summit. They reached the top without further incident, but Viesturs regretfully views their decision to continue on as a mistake, an unnecessary risk—the only major blemish in his mountaineering career.

page 19

Smoky Mountains

Galen Rowell/Mountain Light

Dark gray river stones dot a still creek while bright green leaves mix with fall foliage— a tranquil autumn retreat off Virginia's Blue Ridge Parkway. A haven for campers, picnickers, scenic drivers, and hikers, the Blue Ridge Parkway is over four hundred miles long, and ends at the foot of Great Smoky Mountains National Park in western Virginia.

pages 20–21

Eastern Sierra Nevada Mountains

Galen Rowell/Mountain Light

Sunlight illuminates winter's barren landscape, casting a curtain of gold across Buttermilk Road, visually separating it— at least briefly—from the stormy blue-gray of California's Basin Mountain, part of the Eastern Sierra. Named at the turn of the twentieth century for the area's then-productive dairy farming, the road leads into the high desert before abruptly ending at the High Sierra crest.

page 23

Northwest California

Glenn Oakley

Cyclists escape into the lush rolling hills of an Arcata, California, biking trail.

pages 24–25

Aspen, Colorado

Galen Rowell/Mountain Light

Delicate mustard wildflowers dot the banks of Maroon Bells Lake, contrasting beautifully with the red-capped Rocky Mountains above. This gorgeous retreat, near Aspen, Colorado, offers spectacular alpine lakes, whispering rows of aspen trees, and glorious trails to accommodate horses and foot-hikers, making it one of the most popular vacation spots in the state.

pages 26–27

Death Valley

Ted Delker

Miles of glowing, rippling sand dunes stretch on in the distance, giving a rare, exhilarating view of the vast and fiery Death Valley, part of the Southwest's Mojave Desert and a favorite wintertime escape.

page 28

Southwestern Wyoming

Galen Rowell/Mountain Light

The sun dips below Mount Hooker's towering 2,000-foot granite wall, turning its face burnt-orange. Tucked away in Wind River Range, Wyoming, Mount Hooker offers solitude and expert climbing to those seeking refuge and challenge.

page 29

Mount Whitney, California

Galen Rowell/Mountain Light

A hiker gazes at the steep, formidable east face of Mount Whitney, the highest mountain in the lower forty-eight United States at 14,494 feet. Mount Whitney has a 2,000-foot granite wall that is one of the most continuous faces in the High Sierra, making it a popular ascent, both for moderate climbers and day-hikers. Ironically, Mount Whitney is located only eighty-five miles from the lowest point in the United States, Badwater Basin (-279 ft.) in Death Valley.

pages 42–43
Colorado
Dennis Wiand

With the dazzling Rocky Mountains as a backdrop, a family winds down after a day of camping and hiking in Governor Basin, Colorado. Governor Basin, just an hour-long jeep ride from Ouray, is also located near the old mining towns of Sneffels and Camp Bird.

page 44
Smoky Mountains
Glenn Oakley

Breaking trail for his group to follow, a ski guide trudges through the powdery terrain of Idaho's Smoky Mountains, testing snow conditions following a severe storm.

page 47
Central Idaho
Glenn Oakley

Backcountry skiers carve sweeping, rounded turns on Galena Pass, Idaho, making hours of uphill climbing worth the work. Windswept Galena Pass, elevation 8,000 feet, is located north of famed Sun Valley. With multiple ranges spreading from it in every direction, the mountain is often the starting point for powder-hungry skiers and snowboarders.

pages 48–49
Northwest Territories, Canada
Galen Rowell/Mountain Light

Fall colors and green moss decorate the edge of a dry pond near the head of the Thelon River in the Barrens, the tundra of northern Canada's sub-Arctic. Despite the climate, the Barrens, which covers the area from the polar sea to the southern tree line, supports myriad plant and animal life.

page 50
Mount McKinley, Alaska
Galen Rowell/Mountain Light

A mountaineer descends from Mount McKinley, walking in frigid temperatures toward Peters Glacier. Mount McKinley, Alaska, is the highest point on the North American continent—20,320 feet—and has been called one of the last great wild places in that part of the world.

page 53
Northwest Territories, Canada
Galen Rowell/Mountain Light

A fine autumn mist creeps in and out of fir trees at dawn, hovering over the headwaters of the Thelon River. This part of the river is 250 miles from the nearest road, in the heart of Canada's rugged Northwest Territories.

pages 54–55
Sierra Nevada Mountains
Galen Rowell/Mountain Light

Sunflowers seem to stretch their faces to the coming dawn in this gold-filled meadow at the foot of the White Mountains in Owens Valley, California. The semi-arid region— flocked by the Sierra Nevada Mountains to the west and the White and Inyo Mountains to the east—is just miles from Mammoth Mountain, one of California's most popular ski resorts.

pages 56–57
Oregon
David Jensen

A backpacker winds through the rocky hills that make up Hell's Canyon. Flanked by the Snake River, which splits the canyon into two distinct parts, Hell's Canyon encompasses the borders of Oregon and Idaho. Both the canyon trails and the river make this enormous 213,993-acre canyon a popular warm-weather destination for white-water rafting, hiking, and camping.

pages 60-61
Eagle Cap Wilderness, Oregon
David Jensen

Swirling curlicues and lily-pad shapes decorate a swamp lake in Eagle Cap Wilderness, Oregon. This breathtaking national refuge is marked by high alpine lakes and meadows, and plenty of wildlife, with almost forty miles of river and over fifty lakes for trout fishing. To preserve the beauty of Eagle Cap, visitors must pack out what they bring in, and disassemble any permanent structures they create—such as fire rings—when leaving.

pages 62–63
Glen Canyon, Arizona
John Elk

A hiker is dwarfed by the towering rock that characterizes Coyote Gulch, a popular hike in the Escalante Canyons. The Escalante River meanders through some of the most remote, beautiful country in the Southwest. This backcountry, part of Utah's Glen Canyon, provides a valuable respite for travelers seeking peace from the crowded—but grand—Lake Powell nearby.

page 59
Eastern California
Galen Rowell/Mountain Light

A natural arch of eroded granite in the Alabama Hills of Owens Valley, California, provides a stunning peek-hole view of Mount Whitney, at right, and Lone Pine Peak, at left.

page 64
Concord, Massachusetts
Galen Rowell/Mountain Light

Bright red and yellow fall leaves sprinkle the still waters of this Waldenesque pond in Concord, Massachusetts, mirroring the full spectrum of New England fall colors found in Punkatesset Woods nearby.

 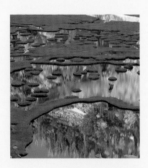  

page 67
Idaho
Glenn Oakley

Descending from Titus Peak, Idaho, a backcountry enthusiast etches the first turns of the day. Backcountry skiing has recently become more popular, as resorts from New Mexico to British Columbia have opened previously off-limits terrain to fresh-powder seekers willing to risk the hypothermia, avalanche, and injury that often mar off-piste adventure.

page 69
Hawaii
© Beverly Factor/ImageState

A large green sea turtle floats in Hawaii's clear ocean waters.

page 70
Northern Arizona
© Charles S. Munsey/ImageState

Sunlight filters through the rippling sandstone walls of Antelope Canyon in Arizona, located near Lake Powell. Widely regarded as one of the most hauntingly beautiful slot canyons in the country, Antelope Canyon—nearly five miles long in its entirety—is noted among photographers for the way the sandstone brilliantly absorbs and reflects the sun.

page 71
Zion National Park, Utah
David Jensen

The deep rock walls of the Narrows in Zion National Park make for a picturesque yet challenging hike. The Narrows, one of Zion's best-known natural wonders, is a 2,000-foot chasm that, over thousands of years, was carved by the Virgin River's fickle and often-rough waters. The hike through the river is difficult, since it is trail-less—hikers must tread directly through the water—but the payoff of seeing Zion's gorgeous canyons, rock formations, and rugged backcountry is phenomenal.

pages 72-73
Eastern Washington
Tom Burkhart

Paddling in the late afternoon sunlight, the Cascade Mountains looming in the distance, a group of kayakers take in the exquisite, rugged beauty of Cooper Lake, Washington.

page 74
Sierra Nevada Mountains
Galen Rowell/Mountain Light

In a secluded High Sierra alcove above North Lake, a quaking aspen has turned vivid red in October, going far beyond the normal fall color-shift from green to yellow to rival the richest hues seen in the forests of New England.

page 77
Arches National Park, Utah
Galen Rowell/Mountain Light

With a coal-gray, stormy sky and orange sandstone as inspiration, a runner travels along the trail to Delicate Arch in Utah's Arches National Park, where every turn and trail seems to lead to a more exhilarating landscape. Located near Moab, Arches National Park features one of the world's largest collections of natural sandstone arches, along with other incredible geologic formations including spires, pinnacles, pedestals, and balanced rocks.

pages 78–79
Southeastern Oregon
David Jensen

Perched above Wild Horse Lake in southeastern Oregon, a hiker drinks in the tranquil aquamarine water, outlined by the sparse but serene green hills that make up Steens Mountain. The mountain, a thirty-mile fault block, stands as a stark contrast to Oregon's otherwise lush plant life, and is a popular destination for scenic driving.

page 80
Great Basin National Park, Nevada
Galen Rowell/Mountain Light

A turn through the red-rock walls of Lehman Caves in Great Basin National Park, Nevada, reveals a stunning display of stalagmites, columns, and flow rock. Lehman Caves— just one cavern despite its name—delves a quarter of a mile into the limestone and marble beneath the Snake Range.

page 83
Carlsbad Caverns, New Mexico
Tom Till

Hundreds of limestone stalagmites cover the floor of Carlsbad Caverns in New Mexico, one of the country's largest, most spectacular—and famous—caves. Though known primarily for its caving, Carlsbad Caverns National Park also contains seemingly endless miles of primitive hiking trails that wind through rugged, solitary wilderness.

pages 84–85
Banff National Park, Alberta, Canada
Barbara Cushman Rowell/Mountain Light

A gathering of canoes, docked in Moraine Lake, enhance the spellbinding scenery that draws visitors in droves to Banff National Park in southwestern Canada. Though millions of outdoor enthusiasts visit the park each year, its diverse and enormous 7,000-kilometer landscape makes it possible to climb, kayak, hike, camp, and sightsee in near solitude.

page 86
Bay Area, Northern California
Galen Rowell/Mountain Light

The converging kelly-green foothills of Mount Diablo recede into the distance on a spring afternoon near Morgan Territory Regional Preserve in Contra Costa County, east of San Francisco Bay. Mount Diablo is the dominant peak of the San Francisco Bay Region, and is just one of the stunning natural landscapes characteristic of Northern California's Bay Area.

page 87
Sierra Nevada Mountains
Galen Rowell/Mountain Light

The sun creeps over the ridge of the Eastern Sierra Nevada Mountains, highlighting a cluster of orangey-yellow aspen trees blessed with fall's Midas touch.

pages 88–89
Great Smoky Mountains National Park, Tennessee
Galen Rowell/Mountain Light

The thick, lush interior of this hardwood forest in Great Smoky Mountains National Park, Tennessee, provides a refreshing experience of solitude and renewal. The trees that make up forests such as these grow at a higher elevation than any other deciduous forest in the East.

pages 90–91
Mount McKinley, Alaska
Galen Rowell/Mountain Light

A mountaineer soaks in the view from the summit of Mount McKinley, gazing at an endless sea of clouds and nearby peaks. Also widely known as "Denali," Mount McKinley each year attracts thousands of climbers willing to brave the frigid temperatures and avalanche hazards in order to reach the summit.

pages 92–93
Joshua Tree National Park, California
Don Johnston Images, Inc.

Poised on a sheer face of rock in Joshua Tree National Monument, a climber anticipates his next handhold.

page 95
Rio Santa Maria, Mexico
Glenn Oakley

With undulated force, Tamul Falls—the site where the Rio Gallinas meets the Rio Santa Maria—crashes into the river below, while a nearby kayaker struggles to stay afloat. At 315 feet, Tamul Falls is massive, and with gorgeous jungle scenery along the way, it is one of Mexico's finest whitewater experiences, and a popular destination for many kayaking trips.

page 96
Arizona
© Dugald Bremner/ImageState

Mustard-yellow grasses ripple through an Arizona meadow, transforming an otherwise ordinary mountain biking route into a luminous trail of gold.

page 97
Rio Tampaon, Mexico
Glenn Oakley

Two kayakers, cradled in a deep canyon ravine, paddle the bright blue—and surprisingly calm—waters of the Rio Tampaon in Mexico. Mexico has some of the most intriguing and least paddled whitewater rivers in the world.

page 98
Northern California
Galen Rowell/Mountain Light

Dangling over the cold Pacific Ocean with acrobatic grace, a climber painstakingly inches up what is known as the "Endless Bummer," a climb on Mickey's Beach, near Stinson Beach on California's Marin County coast.

page 101
Truckee River, California
© Larry Proser

With verve, a kayaker navigates the surging waters of the Truckee River, near Lake Tahoe in Northern California. The river was named after a Native American—dubbed "Captain Truckee" by early settlers—who led the first wagon train across Donner Pass into California.

pages 102–103
Eastern Oregon
David Jensen

A cross-country skier, gliding through a mass of fresh white powder, traverses the Elkhorn Crest Trail above Anthony Lake in eastern Oregon, one of the most scenic and best-maintained trails in that part of the state. The trail offers dazzling views of six different lakes, along with an incredible panorama of the Blue Mountains to the south and west, and Baker Valley and the Wallowa Mountains to the east. In addition to hiking and cross-country travel, the area features rest stops and campsites, and the chance to spot wildlife such as deer, elk, and mountain goats.

pages 104–105
South Dakota
© Parallel Productions/ImageState

A couple wades with determination through a gentle South Dakota stream, hoisting their mountain bikes over their shoulders to reach the long, winding trails on the other side.

page 107
Alaska
© Larry Proser

Gliding through water smooth as glass, a kayaker approaches a looming mountain on Alaska's Prince William Sound. One of the world's best sea kayaking destinations, Prince William Sound is protected from the Gulf of Alaska by the Chugach and Kenai Mountains, making the waters tame— perfect for novice paddlers. The area is also known for its abundant wildlife, and it is common to spot whales, eagles, salmon, and bears.

page 108
Massachusetts
Galen Rowell/Mountain Light

A canopy of sugar maple spread their branches, displaying gorgeous New England fall color over a quiet pond on the outskirts of Massachusetts's Punkatesset Woods, near Concord.

page 109
Columbia River Gorge, Oregon
Glenn Oakley

Windsurfers glide in and out of the waves of the Columbia River Gorge in Hood River, Oregon, their colorful sails rippling in the breeze—a dance in the wind. This spectacular river canyon, known as the windsurfing capital of the Northwest, is eighty miles long and up to 4,000 feet deep. It features the largest concentration of waterfalls in the region along with hundreds of hiking trails and campsites, making it a recreational haven.

page 111
Upper Alaska Peninsula
Galen Rowell/Mountain Light

Like tiny mushrooms, a half-dozen tents dot the bank of Alaska's McNeil River, looking cozy under an impressive canopy of purple-shaded sky. Aside from providing superb camping, McNeil River offers incomparable wildlife observation. Each season, dozens of bears—protected by the government-run McNeil Sanctuary—gather at McNeil Falls to feast on salmon. Those who are lucky enough to obtain viewing permits witness the largest gathering of brown bears in the world.

pages 112–113
Oregon
David Jensen

The blue-green Snake River slithers through the golden, rocky hills of Hell's Canyon, Oregon, captivating a backpacker from his high perch. Though the waters below appear tranquil, Snake River is actually turbulent and raucous—providing the perfect ingredients for whitewater adventure.

page 114
Sierra Nevada Mountains
© Larry Proser

Determined to reach the perfect riding terrain, a man hoists his mountain bike on his back and slowly climbs the steep bank of the Yuba River in California's Sierra Nevada Mountains.

page 117
Eastern Sierra Nevada Mountains
Ted Delker

A couple of mountain bikers blaze through the wooded trail that flanks lower Rock Creek, halfway between Bishop and Mammoth in the Eastern Sierra Nevada Mountains. The trail is one of the area's best-kept secrets. Winding alongside the creek as it descends some 3,000 feet in elevation, it progresses from shaded pines into a rocky gorge. The gorge section provides challenges for experienced riders, and the lack of traffic makes mountain bikers feel as if they truly own the trail.

pages 118–119
Boise, Idaho
Glenn Oakley

Icy blue hoarfrost and heavy fog drape a tree-lined trail in the foothills of Boise, Idaho, transforming a runner's early-morning routine into an inspirational adventure. This hoarfrost is created when a layer of warm air traps the frigid air in the Boise valley, creating an authentic winter wonderland.

pages 120–121
Grand Teton Mountains
Glenn Oakley

Backcountry skiers perch on a cornice bowl high above Jackson Valley, Wyoming, studying their potential route. The jagged, perennially snow-capped peaks of the Grand Tetons lure alpinists, backcountry and free skiers, and summit seekers from all over the world, mesmerizing them with its steep, harsh terrain and starkly beautiful scenery.

page 122
Salmon River, Idaho
Glenn Oakley

Paddle rafters tackle the unpredictable waters of the Salmon River's middle fork, in Idaho. This pristine river—one of America's premier wilderness river trips—offers ever-changing rapids marked by both wide and narrow gorges, along with fabulous hiking trails and a plethora of sparkling hot springs.

page 124
Kings Canyon National Park, California
Galen Rowell/Mountain Light

Hovering over a flame as the sun dips below the mountains, a camper prepares for a frigid winter night in California's Kings Canyon National Park, en route to skiing the 211-mile John Muir Trail, which begins at the top of Mount Whitney and ends in Yosemite Valley. Unlike Yosemite, both Kings Canyon and nearby Sequoia National Park remain unspoiled and relatively quiet, rare places of natural beauty and refuge.

page 125
Eagle Cap Wilderness, Oregon
David Jensen

Pitch by pitch, climbers tackle ice and freezing temperatures on a winter climb in Eagle Cap Wilderness, Oregon. Eagle Cap is home to the Wallowa Mountains, elevation 10,000 feet. Although this national preserve can be subject to sweltering temperatures during the summer, snow often remains on the mountain peaks until August.

pages 126–127
Colorado
Dennis Wiand

Surrounded by Quartz Monzonite rock, hikers gather near the Blue Lakes Trailhead, about an hour from Ouray, Colorado. Though difficult for the first several miles, the hike leads to Colorado's beautiful Blue Lakes, where the camping is abundant, the fishing can be great, and the alpine scenery is spectacular.

pages 128–129
Sierra Nevada Mountains
Galen Rowell/Mountain Light

Cattle graze in Owens Valley, California, unaware that the sunrise has transformed the snow-capped Sierra Nevada Mountains, above, into an awe-inspiring sight of burnished gold.

page 131
Central Utah
Galen Rowell/Mountain Light

An early evening thunderstorm gathers over the San Rafael Swell. Located in the heart of Utah, the San Rafael Swell is a wild and starkly beautiful canyon area, with miles of backcountry hiking and sightseeing—and plenty of solitude.

page 132
Northeastern California
Galen Rowell/Mountain Light

A lenticular cloud hovers over Owens Valley, California, covering the sky with a kaleido-scope of purple, orange, pink, and yellow, reflecting its dramatic beauty on the quiet river below. These thin, lens-shaped clouds can stretch over fifty miles, like the one pictured below. Called the "Sierra Wave" by locals, these clouds are created when high winds force moist air from the Pacific Ocean over the crest of the Sierra Nevada Mountains, pushing the air into an atmosphere so high that the moisture condenses into clouds that mimic the shape of the mountains.

page 133
Grand Canyon National Park, Arizona
© *Charles P. Gurche/ImageState*

The silver-white waters of Havasu Falls tumble one hundred feet into a spectacular pool of turquoise. An oasis in the Grand Canyon, Havasu Canyon's riverbed is lined with limestone, which reflects the sun and gives the surrounding water its exquisite hue.

page 135
Alaska
Galen Rowell/Mountain Light

A macro shot of tiny mushrooms renders them as giants dwarfing the dense coastal foliage in Kachemak Bay, near Homer, Alaska.

pages 136–137
Northeastern California
Ted Delker

The late afternoon sun casts soft light on the pumpkin-orange cottonwood trees sur-rounding Mill Pond, near Bishop, California.

page 138
Maine
Galen Rowell/Mountain Light

Brilliant autumn leaves beautifully frame a trickling waterfall in Smalls Falls, Maine, their bright reds, yellows, and greens an eye-popping contrast to the dark rock. A popular destination for day trips, Smalls Falls offers numerous soothing waterfalls, natural swimming holes, and relaxing picnic areas, and is only minutes from the campsites at Rangeley Lake State Park.

page 139
Everglades National Park, Florida
Galen Rowell/Mountain Light

Sunrise silhouettes a misty thicket of trees· and large ferns in Long Pine Key, Florida, casting an otherworldly crimson haze. Long Pine Key, part of Pinelands in Everglades National Park, is an area of pine forest that grows atop limestone bedrock elevated about two feet above the seasonal flooding. Nearby Rock Reef Pass, the highest point in the national park, is just three feet above sea level. These tree islands are home for many large animals of the Everglades.

page 141

Olympia, Washington
Rob Hansen

This log bridge provides for a picturesque—and undoubtedly for some, nerve-wracking—traverse over the roaring waters of Sol Duc Falls, in Olympia, Washington. With its lush and dense forests, Sol Duc Falls features unforgettable hiking and sightseeing, and is a short drive from a spectacular rainforest in the Hoh River Valley.

pages 142–143

Everglades National Park, Florida
Galen Rowell/Mountain Light

Miles of swaying chartreuse grass stretch on in the distance as pinkish-gray clouds dot the horizon of Sawgrass Prairie in Everglades National Park, Florida. Known as the "River of Grass," the Everglades—a prime camping destination—actually contains myriad ecosystems, including expansive sawgrass, diverse pinelands, and windswept sandy beaches.

page 144

Yosemite National Park, California
Ted Delker

A fresh blanket of snow covers Yosemite Valley, giving the famous park a pristine glow—a rare, beautiful glimpse of early-morning solitude.

page 147

Yellowstone National Park, Montana
Galen Rowell/Mountain Light

A family of elk gathers in a hot springs mist in Yellowstone National Park, Montana. Sometimes called the "Crown Jewel" of national parks for wildlife sightings, Yellowstone offers memorable encounters with animals such as elk, bear, sandhill cranes, osprey, and wolves.

pages 148-149

Eastern Sierra Nevada Mountains
Galen Rowell/Mountain Light

Fall yellow rabbitbrush and tan grasses contrast with the cotton-candy clouds above Mono Lake at sunset. Mono Lake, located in California's Eastern Sierra Nevada Mountains, has changed dramatically over time. Scientists believe that up until 20,000 years ago, the lake was many times its present size, fed by glaciers that descended from Yosemite's Tioga Pass.

page 150

Eastern Washington
Tom Burkhart

A fly-fisherman casts his rod into the still waters of Tucquala Lake, a beautiful and remote area near Cle Elum, Washington.

page 151

Yosemite National Park, California
Galen Rowell/Mountain Light

A tranquil stream zigzags through a hanging meadow on Mount Conness, a 12,590-foot peak in Yosemite National Park. One of the park's most popular trails, Mount Conness Loop takes backpackers through twenty-five miles of rugged and widely varied mountain landscape. Pictured is a trail-less canyon.

page 153

Glacier National Park, Montana
Galen Rowell/Mountain Light

Silver-tinted water cascades from two unnamed falls in Glacier National Park near Logan Pass, parting to reveal a shimmering creek, silhouetted mountains, and rugged purple rock—a mesmerizing world cast in dawn's muted light. Widely called the most pristine of all America's national parks, Glacier is tucked away on Montana's northwestern border, just a few minutes from Canada. It offers over 700 miles of hiking, spectacular sights, and unparalleled scenic drives, most notably Going-to-the-Sun road.

page 154
Sierra Nevada Mountains
Galen Rowell/Mountain Light

The sun creeps up over North Palisade in the High Sierra, revealing a piercing blue sky as a mountaineer gears up for a day of backcountry adventure.

page 155
Yosemite National Park, California
Galen Rowell/Mountain Light

Ski mountaineers prepare for a cold night beneath Cathedral Peak in the Yosemite backcountry, near the end of a seventeen-day, 211-mile traverse of the famous John Muir Trail. John Muir Trail is heavily traveled for the first few miles, but farther in it increasingly becomes a haven for solitude, boasting craggy mountaintops, gleaming lakes, and wildflower meadows.

pages 156–157
Knik River, Alaska
Galen Rowell/Mountain Light

Sunset casts a surreal, enchanting light on the Knik River in Alaska, near Anchorage. The word *knik* is derived from an Eskimo name that means "fire," an appropriate description of the red and yellow hues reflecting on the water below.

page 158
Palomar Mountains, California
Rob Hansen

A late afternoon mist seeps through the bare branches of oak trees that line a highway in Southern California's Palomar Mountains, casting an eerie yet calming effect. Palomar Mountain State Park, just a few hours outside of San Diego, is a popular getaway for those seeking a Sierra Nevada landscape—without the long drive.

pages 160–161
Northwest Territories, Canada
Galen Rowell/Mountain Light

Sunset turns the landscape red as a traveler—250 miles from the nearest road—drinks in the calm and color above a series of lakes at the headwaters of the Thelon River in the Barrens, part of Canada's Northwest Territories. Though the tundra that makes up most of its scenery is sparse, the Barrens's wide-open vistas and abundant wildlife make traveling there richly rewarding.

pages 176–177
Mesa Verde National Park, Colorado
Jim Hamilton Photography

A lone pine tree stands against a dramatic sunset in Mesa Verde National Park, Colorado. At 7,000 feet, this archaeological preserve has several hiking trails that offer sweeping views of the Navajo and Spruce Canyons and rare glimpses of ancient art carved into stone. Due to the land's fragility, however, backcountry hikes and travel are not permitted.

page 179
Sierra Nevada Mountains
Galen Rowell/Mountain Light

Summer blooms of lupines and paintbrush grace Minaret Summit at sunset as the spires of the Minarets pierce the evening sky. The range's bluish-black color comes from meta-volcanics that line the more usual light-colored granite of the High Sierra.

page 180
Northern California
Galen Rowell/Mountain Light

A lone oak tree stands in the middle of the Central Valley at dawn in Rancho Cordova, near Sacramento, California.

Foreword by Ed Viesturs

Ed Viesturs is an internationally renowned mountaineer who has climbed many of the world's most challenging summits. He is one of two people to have climbed Mount Everest five times—and the only American and one of just five people to climb the six highest peaks in the world, all without supplemental oxygen. Currently, he is on a quest to climb all fourteen of the world's highest peaks, and has summitted twelve. He is featured in the IMAX film *Everest* and in the 2000 movie *Vertical Limit*.

Ed's passion for climbing began when he was a college student in Washington, where he inaugurated a long-running obsession with Mount Rainier. He landed a guide job there in the summers, and continued to work at Rainier during his four years of veterinary study. After several years of juggling climbing and a veterinary career, however, the call of the mountains won out. A professional climber, Ed now lives with his wife and two children in Seattle.

Introduction by Page Stegner

Page Stegner is a novelist, critic, and the author of four books on the American West, including *Outposts of Eden*, *American Places* (with Wallace Stegner and Eliot Porter), and *Grand Canyon: The Great Abyss*. He is professor (emeritus) of literature at the University of California, Santa Cruz, where among his many honors he has been the recipient of a National Endowment in the Humanities, a National Endowment in the Arts, and a Guggenheim Fellowship. Page lives with his wife and daughter in Shelburne, Vermont.

Peter Oliver

Peter Oliver is a contributing editor of *Skiing* magazine and a contributor to a number of other publications on outdoor adventure. His fifth book, *Skiing & Snowboarding*, is part of *Outside* magazine's new adventure-travel series. He lives in Warren, Vermont, and when not traveling to mountains around the world, skis mostly at nearby Sugarbush and Mad River Glen.

Pamela Hunt

Pamela Hunt grew up in Pennsylvania where running trails are abundant! She ran on Cornell University's cross-country and track teams and competed in the 1991 and 1992 World Cross-Country Championships on the U.S. Junior Team. Pamela traded in the mountains for the oceans and canyons of San Diego, where she now lives and runs. She works as a copywriter for Alden Associates.

Melanie Beroth Dobson

Melanie Beroth Dobson is an independent publicist and author of the book for single women *Latte for One and Loving It*. She spends her weekends exploring both above and below the ground outside her hometown of Colorado Springs.

Jeanhee Kim

Jeanhee Kim is a journalist and a director of interactive media in New York City. In her free time, she is an avid swimmer, volleyball player, scuba diver, and all-around fun-seeker.

Rob Story

Rob Story writes about adventure travel and sports for a variety of halfway decent magazines, including *Outside*, *Men's Journal*, and *Rolling Stone*. He's the author of *Outside Adventure Travel: Mountain Biking* (W.W. Norton). Rob lives in Telluride, Colorado.

Bobbie Conlan

Bobbie Conlan, freelance writer and editor and former managing editor of Time-Life Books, is a displaced Hawaiian who kayaks on the Potomac River near Washington, D.C.

Jeremy Schmidt

Writer Jeremy Schmidt lived in Yellowstone for six years during the 1970s. He had a variety of jobs, ranging from park ranger to plumber, but the best was winterkeeper—winter caretaker—at Old Faithful. He recalls, "I had a friend, a poet, who sent her letters to 'The Old Faithful Keeper of Winter.' She said someone had to keep it, after all, and although I wasn't particularly old, she thought I'd do the job faithfully. I tried to." Jeremy now lives in Jackson Hole, Wyoming, and writes about wild areas around the world.

Susan Zwinger

Susan Zwinger is the noted author of numerous books, articles, and essays on wildlife and wilderness protection. She also teaches workshops in natural history, natural history writing, advanced writing, art, and illustrated journaling. She lives and wanders the wild beaches on an island north of Seattle.

Galen Rowell/Mountain Light Photography

Galen Rowell is an award-winning fine art, landscape, and outdoor adventure photographer based in Bishop, California. In 1972, he began his career as a full-time photographer and writer, and after less than a year, landed his first major magazine assignment—a cover story for *National Geographic*. Further assignments and private expeditions have taken him to both poles and on more than forty other international journeys into Africa, Antarctica, Canada, China, Europe, India, Nepal, New Zealand, Pakistan, Patagonia, Scandinavia, South America, and Tibet. Recent travels have taken him to the Barrens region of the Canadian Arctic, and the Amazon rainforest in Brazil.

In 1984 Galen received the Ansel Adams Award for his contributions to the art of wilderness photography and began teaching photo workshops around the country. He has also produced seventeen large-format books of photos and text. His book *Bay Area Wild* celebrates the wild areas within a forty-mile radius of San Francisco. His most recent book, *Galen Rowell's Inner Game of Outdoor Photography*, is a collection of essays based on his monthly column in *Outdoor Photographer* magazine.

Major exhibitions of his work have been shown at galleries such as The Nikon House and International Center of Photography in New York; The Smithsonian Institution in Washington, D.C.; The Field Museum in Chicago; The Ansel Adams Gallery in Yosemite National Park; The Nature Company's Wrubel Gallery; and The California Academy of Sciences in San Francisco.

When not working on assignment for commercial clients or publications such as *Life, National Geographic, Outdoor Photographer, Audubon,* and *Coastal Living*, Galen is likely to be found either writing at his Bishop home, climbing in the High Sierra, or working with his images at Mountain Light Photography, an agency and fine-art photographic gallery managed by his wife, Barbara, to distribute stock photographs for publication and exhibition prints for sale through galleries and museums. More of Galen's work can be viewed on his website, www.mountainlight.com

Tom Burkhart

Tom Burkhart has traveled worldwide to photograph vehicles for American, European, and Asian clients. He maintains studios in both Michigan and California, but most of the year, he is on location. Tom began his career as a photojournalist after attending the University of Michigan and The Center for Creative Studies.

Ted Delker

Ted Delker is an amateur photographer who for over forty years has traveled throughout the United States with his family, capturing the scenery along the way. Since retiring from Southern California's aerospace industry, Ted and his wife, Judy, have moved to one of their favorite vacation spots: Bishop, California. They now spend a portion of each year exploring the country in their motor home and are currently retracing the path of the Lewis and Clark expedition from St. Louis, Missouri, to Seaside, Oregon.

John Elk

John Elk is half of a husband-and-wife photography team that has traveled to twenty-eight states and nearly fifty countries in North America, Europe, Africa, and Asia. They have a continually expanding stock photography library of 300,000 images and belong to several professional photography organizations. John has been shooting professionally for more than twenty years.

Rob Hansen

Rob Hansen is a free-lance photographer based in Encinitas, California, who works on both fine art and corporate photography. Rob studied studio art at the University of California, Santa Barbara, and at the Art Center College of Design in Pasadena.

David Jensen

David Jensen's interest in adventure photography began at the age of twelve when he climbed Oregon's Mount Hood. Since then he has photographed many of the major peaks of North America and has climbed 20,000-foot mountains in Peru. His photos have appeared in publications ranging from Sierra Club calendars to Time-Life books.

Don Johnston

Don Johnston has always had an affinity for nature and action photography. His work can be found in countless national ads, brochures, calendars, and web sites. Although the primary emphasis of his professional work centers on automotive photography, his images can also be found in ads for watercraft, winter sports, and other outdoor activities. More of Don's work is available at www.johnstonimages.com.

Glenn Oakley

Glenn Oakley photographs the landscape and the people in it for advertising and editorial clients ranging from L.L. Bean to *Smithsonian* magazine. An avid kayaker, canoer, hiker, mountain biker, and skier, Oakley has pursued photographic adventures from the Arctic Ocean to the jungles of Guatemala. More of his work can be seen at www.oakleyphoto.com.

Larry Proser

Larry Proser has had a love affair with the camera since his grandfather handed him one at age twelve. A self-taught photographer, he focuses mainly on what he calls "Man at Play in Nature." This has led to many adventures in various parts of the world, including surfing in Indonesia and powder skiing in Canada. Larry is an active participant in many of the sports he photographs, and often brings along his family for shoots.

Dennis Wiand

Dennis Wiand is a Michigan-based free-lance photographer. His first experience with photography began on a cross-country trip with his high school buddies, using his father's Argus C-3 to shoot scenery out the window of a 1968 Thunderbird. He is a graduate of the Center for Creative Studies in Detroit. Dennis feels fortunate that his clients, advertising agencies representing the major automotive companies, allow him to play in the dirt with cars-his other childhood love.

TREAD LIGHTLY!

Take only memories. Leave only footprints.

*Today we have more freedom than ever for fun and recreation, to travel
and experience the wonders of mountains, beaches, trails, and desert.
Yet with this freedom comes responsibility. As we strive to push our personal
boundaries—whether we're kayaking, mountain biking, backpacking, or skiing—
we must take care to leave nature in the pristine condition in which we
found her. Being environmentally responsible is not difficult. It only requires
common sense, respect, and the commitment to follow some basic principles:*

TRAVEL AND RECREATE WITH MINIMUM IMPACT

❖

RESPECT THE ENVIRONMENT AND THE RIGHTS OF OTHERS

❖

EDUCATE YOURSELF, PLAN, AND PREPARE BEFORE YOU GO

❖

ALLOW FOR FUTURE USE OF THE OUTDOORS, LEAVING IT BETTER THAN YOU FOUND IT

❖

DISCOVER THE REWARDS OF RESPONSIBLE RECREATION

*Nature is a home for rare animals and exotic plant life, and her
beauty is a needed refuge for us all. Each adventure into the wild,
our "outdoor" home, brings a sense of discovery, of renewal—
and a commitment to respect the fragility of the earth.*

treadlightly!®

PARTNER IN EDUCATION

[*For more information about how to be environmentally sensitive as you adventure, visit www.treadlightly.org.*]